L643i

Astrid Lindgren

I WANT TO GO TO SCHOOL TOO

Pictures by Ilon Wikland

Translated by Barbara Lucas

R&S BOOKS

Stockholm　　New York　　London　　Toronto

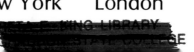

Here are Peter and Lena. Peter is seven years old and goes to school. There he has a teacher. He also has a reading book, a writing book, a counting book, and a pencil box with several fine pencils.

Lena is five years old. She doesn't go to school and she doesn't have a teacher, but she wants one very much.

"I want to go to school too!" Lena says every day.

Lena tries to pretend that she has a teacher, but it would be a lot easier if she knew exactly what happens at school.

Then one morning, guess
what? Peter tells Lena,
"Hurry up and get dressed.
You're coming with me today
to see just what my school
is like."

Lena is so excited and thinks Peter is nice.

Here they are drinking hot chocolate and eating breakfast.

Afterward, they start out for school. Peter has his book bag with him. All his books are in it.

When they cross the street, they have to be careful. A lot of cars are coming and going.

"First you must look to the right, and then to the left, and then to the right again," Peter tells Lena. But Lena is looking only at her brother. How lucky that Peter is used to traffic!

Soon they reach the school. There are almost no children in the schoolyard yet because Peter and Lena left home too early. Only two boys are there — Bo and Jan. They are playing a game of marbles, which Peter joins. Lena stands and watches because she doesn't know how to play.

Peter wins a fine glass marble, which you can see here.

He gives it to Lena.

"This is a nice school!"
says Lena.

Now more and more
children are coming. They
all want to know who Lena is.

"This is my sister," says
Peter. "She wants to go to
school."

The bell rings and all the
children go in — Lena too.

At last Lena gets to see what Peter's teacher looks like. Peter tells the teacher that Lena is his sister. "She wants to know exactly what it's like in school," he explains.

"That's fine!" says the teacher. "Welcome, little Lena."

Lisa, one of the girls in Peter's class, is not in school today because she has a sore throat. So Lena can sit at Lisa's desk. She pretends that it's her own desk. A red duffel bag hangs on one side of it. That's where Lisa keeps her gym clothes.

Lena cannot help but peek inside the desk. There are so many exciting things in there. She pretends that all of them belong to her.

The first hour they study arithmetic. Peter gets to go to the blackboard and add 6 + 4 + 1. Something else is written on the board: *Happy Birthday, Pelle.* The teacher has written it because today is Pelle's birthday. Pelle is the one wearing the red sweater.

During the next hour they have nature study. The teacher shows the children a little stuffed bird, which looks like this.

"Can you guess what kind of bird this is?" she asks.

"A lark," says Bo.

"A swallow," says Inger.

But they are not right.

Lena raises her hand, even though she doesn't really go to school. "I know," she says. "That is a chaffinch."

"Bravo, Lena!" says the teacher.

Peter quickly adds that there are lots of chaffinches where he and Lena stay in the country every summer.

And then Pelle says there are swallows under the eaves at his summer house.

Once, says Jan, a snake came into the garden where he visits in the country. And there's a big gooseberry bush with lots of gooseberries.

"And we also have a cat in the country," says Jan.

"Yes, well, now we must get back to the chaffinch," says the teacher, and she puts a record on the record player. It is the sound of a little chaffinch singing.

Lena thinks nature study is fun.

Then it is lunchtime. Peter takes Lena to the lunchroom.

"I hope we don't get fish today," says Peter, who doesn't like fish.

What luck! It's not fish at all, but pancakes — with lingonberry jam. Lena gets to sit beside Peter at the table.

"I could eat a hundred pancakes," says Inger.

"I could eat thousands," says Bo.

"But I could eat only half of a little, little fish," says Peter.

Lena would like so much to say that she could also eat thousands of pancakes, but she doesn't dare.

It is just as well that Bo doesn't eat thousands of pancakes, because right after lunch the children have gym in the school-yard. How would Bo be able to skip and yell and play wheelbarrow with thousands of pancakes in his stomach?

"Gym is the best thing about school," Peter tells Lena. And Pelle shows her what big muscles you get from gym. He has already forgotten how stupid it is to bring little kids to school.

Lena sits and watches the children.

Here Peter and Lena and all the children are going home.

That evening, Peter is reading a funny book. Lena sits down across from him with a book Mama gave her. She points to the words and reads, "Grandmother is nice . . ."

"Boy, are you dumb," says Peter. "There's not a word about Grandmother in that book. It's all about squirrels."

"It doesn't matter," says Lena. "I will read however I want, because *now* I know exactly what goes on at your school!"

Rabén & Sjögren Stockholm

Text copyright © 1979 by Astrid Lindgren
Pictures copyright © 1979 by Ilon Wikland
Translation copyright © 1987 by Barbara Lucas
All rights reserved
Library of Congress catalog card number: 87-45162
Originally published in Swedish under the title *Jag vill också gå i skolan*
by Rabén & Sjögren, 1979
Printed in Italy
First American edition, 1987

R & S Books are distributed in the United States by Farrar, Straus and Giroux, New York,
in the UK by Ragged Bears, Andover,
and in Canada by Methuen Publications, Toronto, Ontario.
ISBN 91 29 58328 4